When Hugo's mother goes into hospital, he must decide who he wants to stay with. The key to it all is Henry, his dog.

Anne Fine writes her stories in pencil ("a 2B") and then types the final version. "I write a sentence, rub out and go over it again and again until it's absolutely right," she says. Her many books for children include *The Haunting of Pip Parker*, *Bill's New Frock* and *Flour Babies*. She has won the Smarties Book Prize, the Guardian Children's Fiction Award and, on two occasions, the Carnegie Medal and the Whitbread Children's Book Award, most recently for *The Tulip Touch*. She was voted Children's Author of the Year in 1990 and 1993. Her book *Goggle-eyes* was dramatized as a BBC TV serial and *Madame Doubtfire* was turned into the highly successful Hollywood film, *Mrs Doubtfire*. She has two daughters and lives in Edinburgh.

Paul Howard has illustrated a number of stories for Walker, including *Taking the Cat's Way Home*, *One for Me, One For You*, *Friends Next Door*, *A Very Special Birthday* and the picture books *John Joe and the Big Hen*, *Rosie's Fishing Trip*, *The Year in the City*, *Mockingbird* and the anthology *Classic Poetry: an Illustrated Collection*. He is married and lives in London.

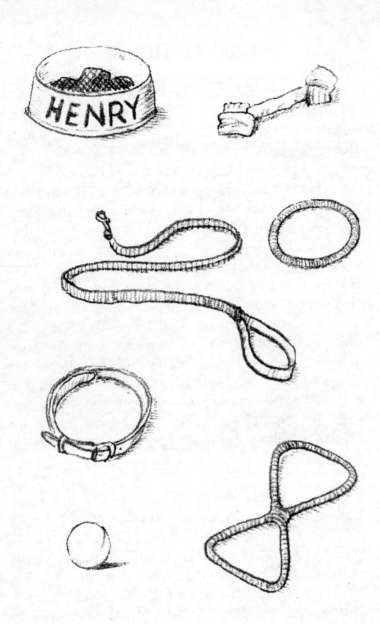

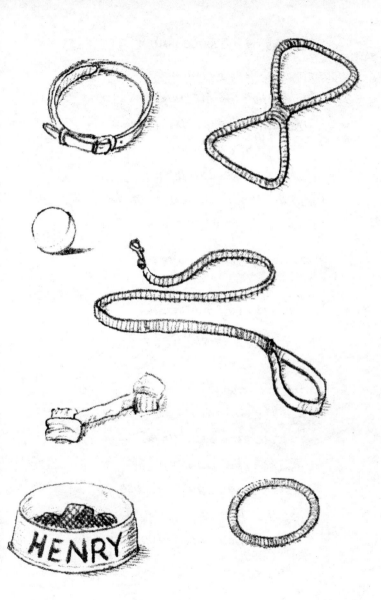

Books by the same author

A Country Pancake

Anneli the Art Hater

The Haunting of Pip Parker

Only a Show

Stranger Danger

A Sudden Puff of Glittering Smoke

For older readers

Bill's New Frock

The Book of the Banshee

Crummy Mummy and Me

Flour Babies

Goggle-eyes

The Granny Project

Madame Doubtfire

The Other Darker Ned

Round Behind the Ice-house

The Stone Menagerie

The Summer-house Loon

ANNE FINE

CARE OF HENRY

Illustrations by Paul Howard

WALKER BOOKS
AND SUBSIDIARIES
LONDON • BOSTON • SYDNEY

For Annie
P.H.

First published 1996 by
Walker Books Ltd, 87 Vauxhall Walk
London SE11 5HJ

This edition published 1997

6 8 10 9 7

This book has been typeset in Garamond.

Printed in England by Clays Ltd, St Ives plc

British Library Cataloguing in Publication Data
A catalogue record for this book
is available from the British Library.

ISBN 0-7445-5258-3

CONTENTS

CHAPTER 1

Hugo's mother was going to have a
baby. Very soon. She kept saying to
Hugo, "I'll only be gone for three
days. I'm not asking you to choose
a new *mother*. Just who you're
going to stay with till I get back. So,
come along, Hugo. Where's it going
to be? Granny's house?"

Hugo just shrugged.

"Next door with
Mrs Mariposa?"
Hugo's face
went blank.

"At Uncle Jack's flat?"
Hugo said nothing.

"How about at a posh five-star hotel, with a telly in the bedroom, and a swimming pool and a jacuzzi, all by yourself?"

"That would be lovely," said Hugo.

"I was joking," said his mother. And she waddled off to take the sheets off the line before it rained.

Hugo sat glumly stroking Henry's
ears, trying to decide. He knew he
was good at choosing some things,
like food, and what to watch on
telly. And he was bad at choosing
others. This was obviously one of
the others.

Just then, the door bell rang.

"That will be someone to look at the house," said Mum. "I hope they buy it."

"So do I," said Hugo (though he didn't look forward to helping to choose the next house).

"Fingers crossed, then," said his mother. And she answered the door.

On the step was a man with a clipboard and a pencil.

"Nice freshly painted front door," he said, and made a little mark on the paper on his clipboard.

He stepped inside.

"Fine airy hall," he said, and marked his paper again.

Hugo and Henry showed him round the house. In every room, he stood and looked, and then marked his paper. Hugo and Henry watched him.

"What are you writing?" asked Hugo. "Is it ticks and crosses for good and bad, like in school?"

The man looked a bit embarrassed. "And blanks," he said. "If it's nothing special, I just leave a blank."

"How are we doing?" asked Hugo.

The man held the clipboard to his chest, so Hugo couldn't see it. "Fine," he said heartily. "Just fine."

Hugo was interested. "So, if you put all ticks, you might buy the house?"

"I might."

"But if it was all crosses, you wouldn't?"

"No, I certainly wouldn't."

"Clever," said Hugo. "Very, very clever."

They went into the garden. The man helped Hugo's mother fold the two big sheets. And then he said goodbye.

At the gate, he tripped over Henry and dropped the paper. Hugo picked it up.

"There are blanks on it," Hugo said to him. "And some crosses. Tell me exactly what was wrong, because Mum will want to know."

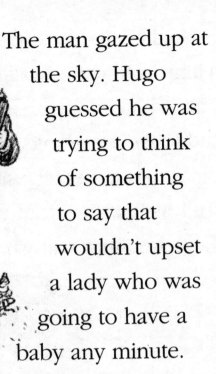

The man gazed up at the sky. Hugo guessed he was trying to think of something to say that wouldn't upset a lady who was going to have a baby any minute. In the end he said, "I think maybe some of the cupboards were a little too spacious."

Hugo went back to his mother.

"He won't buy it," he told her. "He's looking for something with a little less cupboard space."

Hugo's mother stared at the man's back as he walked away. Then she clutched her stomach suddenly.

"You're going to have to hurry up and decide," she told Hugo. "This baby won't wait much longer. Neither will I."

"All right," said Hugo testily. "Don't rush me. Don't rush me."

CHAPTER 2

Hugo phoned his granny. He put
his new clipboard on the table first,
and made sure he had three pencils,
in case two broke.

Then he punched the number.

Granny answered. "Hello. This is
six, four, six, six, seven, seven."

"You shouldn't say that," Hugo told her sternly. "You're not supposed to give out your number like that."

"I've always thought that was ridiculous," his granny said. "If people didn't already know your number, they couldn't have phoned you, could they?"

Hugo decided to start all over again. "Is that you, Granny?"

"Yes. Is that you, Hugo?"

"Yes, it is."

"How nice to hear from you."

"I had one or two questions," said Hugo, looking at his clipboard.

"Fire away," said his granny.

"If," Hugo said, and then he said it again, even more clearly, in case there should be any doubt, "*if* I came to sleep over at your house when Mummy goes into hospital, what will you feed me?"

He held his pencil over the first space on his sheet of paper, and waited.

The answer took a bit of time to come. Then: "Semolina," said Granny rather frostily. "I expect I should feed you semolina."

"You don't usually feed me semolina," Hugo said, putting a big black cross in Granny's FOOD space.

"You don't usually phone up and check on the menu," Granny said tartly.

"Sorry," said Hugo. "Am I being rude?"

"A little."

Hugo had a think. But he had made his chart, and it had taken him hours. He wasn't going to toss the whole thing over. He thought he'd just press on.

"What about telly?" he asked. "Would you let me watch all my favourite telly shows?"

"Not if they're at the same time as mine."

"Which are your favourites, then?" Hugo asked hopefully.

"*Songs of Praise*," said his granny. "*A Week in Politics. Antiques Roadshow.* And that splendid new documentary on the history of shipbuilding."

Hugo gave Granny a huge black cross for ENTERTAINMENT.

"What about bathtime? Can I have it deep?"

"We're on a water shortage," said Granny. "Five inches maximum, I'm afraid."

"With bubbles?"

"We're clean out of bubbles in this house," Granny said cheerfully.

Hugo gave her a cross for BATHTIME and went on to the next question. "What about school the next day?"

"What about it?"

"Will you let me skip it because Mum's having a baby?"

"No," said Granny.

So Granny got a cross for STRICTNESS too.

Hugo came to the last question. "What about Henry? Can he come?"

"Of course he can come," said
Granny. "He's your dog."

"What will you feed him?"

"Rich meat and potato casserole,"
said Granny. "With wine if he likes
it that way. And leftover chocolate
pudding from the day before. And,
of course, some of your semolina, if
he's still got room."

"And can he sleep on my bed? In case things seem strange away from home for three whole days?"

"Yes. Henry can sleep on your bed," said Granny. "If you come."

"*If* I come," Hugo repeated. Then he said goodbye, and looked at Granny's score. If she were a house, he certainly wouldn't buy her. She had four huge black crosses, no blanks, and her only tick was under CARE OF HENRY.

Hugo sighed.

CHAPTER 3

Hugo went next door with his
clipboard to see Mrs Mariposa.
She was washing the floor, with
the twins crawling after her on all
fours. Behind the twins came the
dog. Behind the dog, the cat.

The gerbils were busy spinning their rusty wheel. The washing machine was groaning. And, on the radio, a man was singing *Nessun dorma*.

"*Nes-sun dor-ma,*" sang Mrs Mariposa. "*Nes-sun dor-ma* tonight!"

Hugo coughed loudly, but she didn't hear. He coughed again. Mrs Mariposa turned round.

"Ah, Yugo!" she sang, twirling round her mop.

Hugo put his foot on it.

"Could I ask you a couple of questions?" he began.

Mrs Mariposa hurled the mop into the corner and took Hugo on her knee. The twins and the dog fought for a place on Hugo's lap. The cat jumped on his shoulder. And Hugo had to lift up his clipboard.

"If I come over when Mum goes into hospital…"

Mrs Mariposa leaped to her feet,
spilling everyone on to the floor.

"Your mother! She is ready to go?"

"No, no," said Hugo. "I'm just
planning."

Mrs Mariposa sat down again.
"Very well," she said. "Plan away,
Yugo."

So Hugo went through the questions on his clipboard. "What will we eat?"

Mrs Mariposa threw her hands up in the air. "Ice-cream! My own special chocolate cake! We will have cherries. Yes! We will have cherries. And pizza. We will have pizza."

She looked horribly worried suddenly. "Yugo," she said. "You do *like* my pizza?"

"Oh, yes," said Hugo. "I love your pizza. I've always loved your pizza."

He gave her a giant tick for FOOD, and went on to the next question. "What about television? What will we watch?"

Mrs Mariposa shrugged. "Broken," she said. "Dead broken. But we never watch it anyway."

It was true. In all the hundreds of times Hugo had been in the house, he'd never seen anyone except the gerbils watching telly. So he gave her a blank for ENTERTAINMENT.

"What about bathtime? Can I have it deep?"

"Deep!" cried Mrs Mariposa. "You will have a bath so deep you need waterwings and a life-guard!"

The twins grabbed at Hugo as if to drag him off right now to have a bath.

"With bubbles?" asked Hugo.

"So many bubbles we won't be able to see you!"

Hugo gave her a tick. "What about strictness?"

Mrs Mariposa put out her hand, lifted his chin, and stared into his eyes. "Yugo," she said, "while you are my guest, my house is your house.

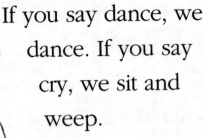

If you say dance, we
dance. If you say
cry, we sit and
weep.

If you say…"

"That's fine,"
said Hugo, and he
gave her a tick.

She had three big ticks already,
but he carried on to
the end.

"And what
about care of
Henry?"

"Henry?"

"Yes," Hugo
said. "Henry."

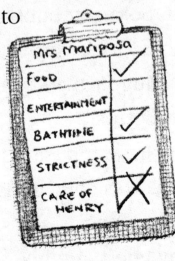

Mrs Mariposa
FOOD	✓
ENTERTAINMENT	
BATHTIME	✓
STRICTNESS	✓
CARE OF HENRY	✗

Mrs Mariposa clapped her hands. "We shall go round to visit Henry every half hour."

"Visit him?" said Hugo. "Can't he come?"

Mrs Mariposa looked around, waving her hands to take in the dog, the cat, the gerbils and the twins. "Remember how it was last time Henry came?"

Hugo remembered. It had taken a full twenty minutes to pick up the broken china and sweep up the fur.

Sadly, he put a big cross under CARE OF HENRY. "Never mind," he told Mrs Mariposa. "It's your only one."

CHAPTER 4

Hugo asked Uncle Jack, "Have you got a pencil?"

Uncle Jack offered him a very flash pen.

"I have a few questions," said Hugo.

"Is it a quiz?" asked Uncle Jack. "I love a good quiz. I'm very good at…"

"Uncle Jack!" Hugo said. "If I come round when Mum goes into hospital, what will we eat?"

"Whatever we fancy," said Uncle Jack. "I don't plan ahead, like you do. If you feel like baked spuds, then that's what we'll have, if I've got any. If you're after something more special, if it's in my book, I'll cook it for you."

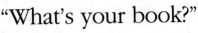

"What's your book?"
"Fast Food For After The Pub,"
said Uncle Jack.
Hugo gave
Uncle Jack a
very faint and
wobbly tick for
FOOD. "Telly?"
he asked.

"Whatever you like, Hugo. I only watch the sport. I'll move it into your bedroom if you like."

Hugo gave him a big tick for ENTERTAINMENT.

"Bathtime? Can I have it deep?"

"Deep as you like. And you can use up all that silly bubble stuff your mother gave me for Christmas."

"*All* of it?"

"All of it," said Uncle Jack firmly, earning another tick.

"What about strictness?"

"Strictness?"

"I mean, will you make me go to school the next day, and all that?"

Uncle Jack stared. "School? What? Get up early and drive you all the way over town just to go to school? You must be mad. It isn't every day your mother has a baby. No, we'll go fishing."

That was one more tick. "And what about Henry?"

"I'll phone the kennels now, to book a place."

Hugo was horrified.

"Kennels? Put Henry in a kennel for days and days?"

"What else can we do?" asked Uncle Jack. "No pets allowed in my flat."

So CARE OF HENRY was his first big cross. And it was such a big one it used up the last of the ink in Uncle Jack's flash pen.

CHAPTER 5

Hugo sat on the doorstep beside Henry. He ran his finger over the sheet of paper on the clipboard.

"Granny has four crosses and one tick," he said. "Mrs Mariposa has three ticks, one blank and one cross. And Uncle Jack has four ticks.

But Mum says the *Fast Food For
After The Pub* book is shocking,
and the faint wobbly tick should be
at least a blank, if not a cross."

He sighed. "That means I should
choose Uncle Jack or Mrs Mariposa.
It all depends on which I really care
about – food or telly."

Henry looked mournful.

"Or you," said Hugo. "If I really care about you, then I should go to Granny's. She's the only one who has a tick under CARE OF HENRY."

They both looked mournful together. Then Hugo said glumly, "Semolina. *A Week in Politics*. Baths five centimetres deep. No bubbles. And school the next day."

He sighed again. "But," he told Henry, "you'll be able to come with me, and you can sleep on my bed."

Henry looked a little more hopeful.

"Have you decided yet?" Hugo's mother asked.

"No," said Hugo. "The ticks on the clipboard say Mrs Mariposa or Uncle Jack. But my heart says Granny."

"Go with your heart," said Mum.

Hugo took hold of Henry by the collar and looked deep into his eyes. "I hope you know I'm doing this for you," he said. "When you're gobbling your rich meat and potato casserole and leftover chocolate pudding, I hope you remember I'm eating semolina for you."

Henry gazed back at him, lovingly.

"And when I'm sitting in my dry bath, and when I'm watching *Songs of Praise*, and when I'm stuck in school, I hope you'll be grateful."

Henry blinked gratefully.

"Very well," Hugo said to his mother. "Granny's it is."

CHAPTER 6

And it wasn't at all bad, really. It turned out that somehow Granny had got mixed up, and made a casserole for Hugo instead of for Henry. (Henry made do with dogfood.)

The leftover chocolate pudding wasn't leftover enough to give to a dog, so Hugo ate that as well. (Henry had a bone.) And there was no semolina.

"Clean out of semolina at the shop," Granny said cheerfully. "But they had plenty of bubble bath."

So Hugo had that. He ran the first few centimetres, then Granny came in and told him he could have all her inches for next week. (That took him up to the overflow.) He stayed in so long, building bubble towers, that he missed *Songs of Praise* and *Antiques Roadshow*.

He went to bed, and Henry slept
with him.

Next day Hugo visited Mum in
hospital. (*After* school.)

And the next day.

And the next.

On the day Mum was coming home, the lady waiting for Mum's bed bumped into Hugo in the corridor. Beside her was the man who came to look at Hugo's house.

"I tried your idea with the clipboard," Hugo told him.

"Did it work?"

"It might have worked," said Hugo. "I won't ever know. Because, in the end, I gave up on ticks and crosses and followed my heart."

"I expect that's the best thing to do," the man said. "I'm having a problem with all the ticks and crosses myself. Maybe I should follow my heart too."

Maybe he did. We'll never know. He didn't buy Hugo's house, anyway.

Hugo's still waiting, and his
sister's *two*.

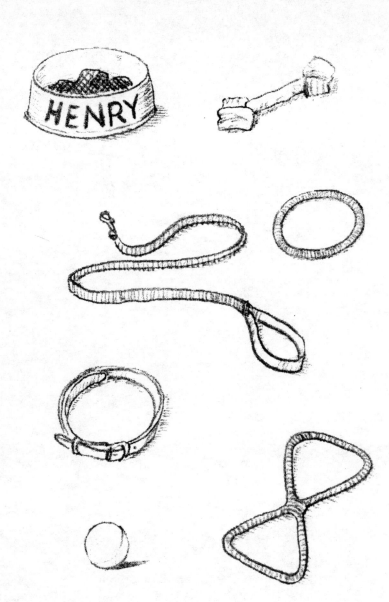

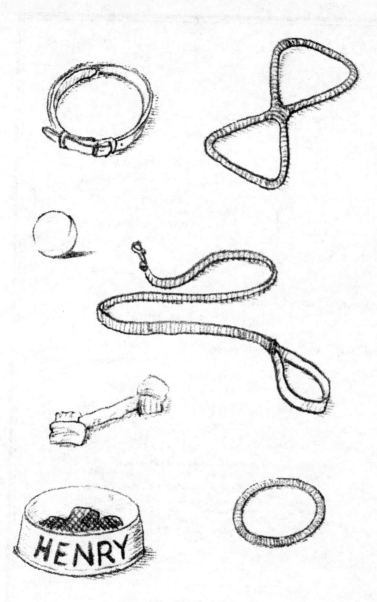

SOME MORE WALKER SPRINTERS
For You to Enjoy

☐ 0-7445-3668-5   *Impossible Parents*
by Brian Patten/Arthur Robins   £3.50

☐ 0-7445-3182-9   *Holly and the Skyboard*
by Ian Whybrow/Tony Kenyon   £3.50

☐ 0-7445-5241-9   *Fort Biscuit*
Lesley Howarth/Ann Kronheimer   £3.50

☐ 0-7445-4739-3   *Posh Watson*
by Gillian Cross/Mike Gordon   £3.50

☐ 0-7445-3188-8   *Beware Olga!*
by Gillian Cross/Arthur Robins   £3.50

☐ 0-7445-4399-2   *Little Stupendo*
Jon Blake/Martin Chatterton   £3.50

☐ 0-7445-3686-3   *The Magic Boathouse*
by Sam Llewellyn/Arthur Robins   £3.50

Name _____

Address _____